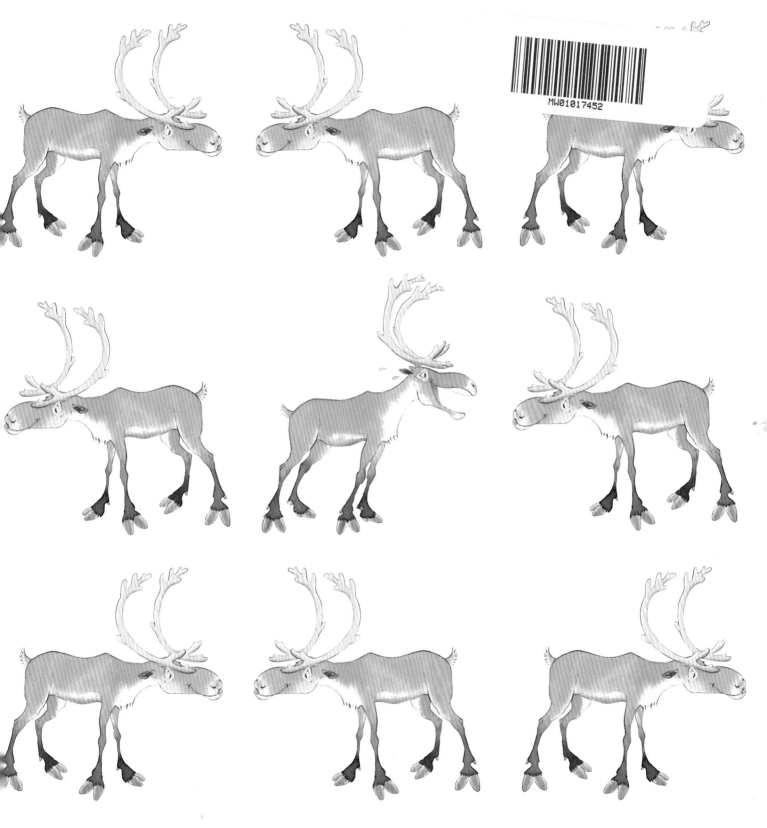

Editor: Nicole Lanctot
Production manager: Louise Kurtz
Designer: Ada Rodriguez

First published in the United States of America in 2015 by Abbeville Press,
137 Varick Street, New York, NY 10013

First published in Belgium in 2015 by Editions Mijade,
18, rue de l'ouvrage, 5000 Namur

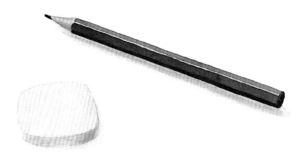

First edition
10 9 8 7 6 5 4 3 2 1

ISBN 978-0-7892-1243-6

Library of Congress Cataloging-in-Publication Data available upon request

For bulk and premium sales and for text adoption procedures, write to Customer
Service Manager, Abbeville Press, 137 Varick Street, New York, NY 10013,
or call 1-800-Artbook.

Visit Abbeville Press online at www.abbeville.com.

Rudy the Reindeer

Sylviane Gangloff

Abbeville Kids
A DIVISION OF ABBEVILLE PRESS
New York · London

Hello! My name is Rudy.

I am a reindeer.

Hey! Who lost a pencil?

It must belong to someone.

Oh! There you are!

Say! Since you're here,
would you mind drawing
something for me?

I would like a pretty forest.

Hey…
that's not a forest!

Please,
I would really like a forest…

with plenty of trees…
if it's not too much trouble.

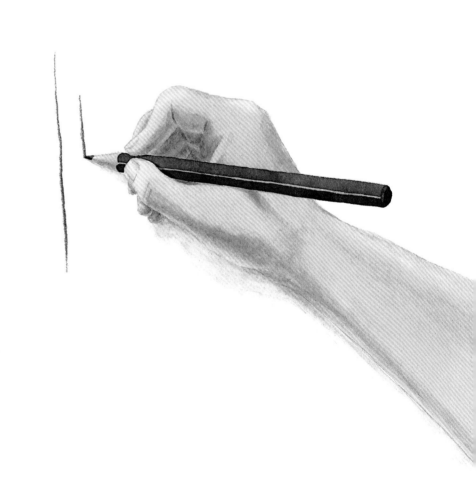

That's very interesting…
but it's not a forest.

Would you, could you, please
draw me a forest?

I'd even settle for a tree.

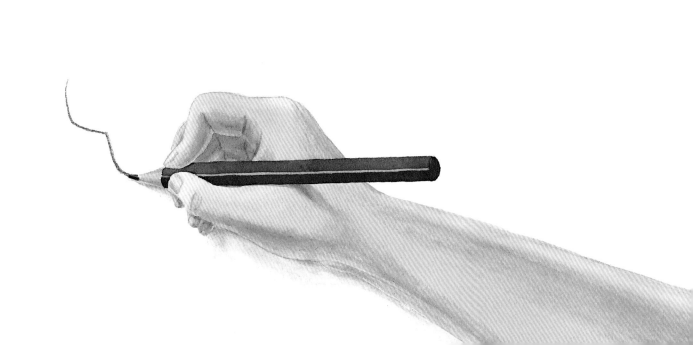

Yikes!
That's not a tree at all!

If this is a joke, it's not one bit funny.

What do you want now?

Oh! Santa Claus!

Santa, you can call me Rudolph.

Thank you for my bright red nose!

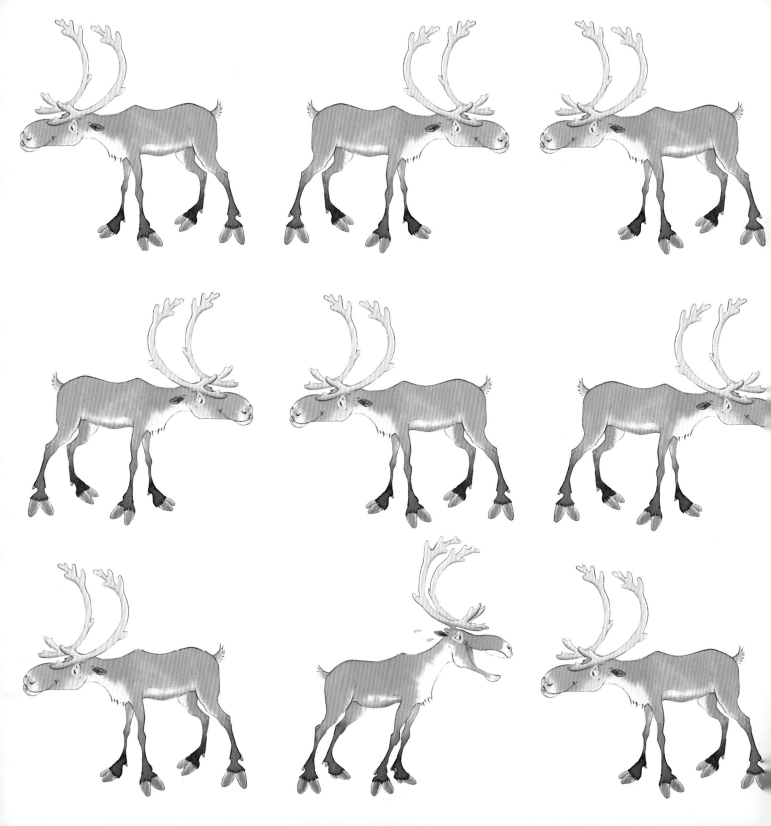